Storyhour Coll.

E   **Hirsh, Marilyn**   c.1

**Potato pancakes all
around**

Do not Circulate

DATE			

POTATO PANCAKES
ALL AROUND
A Hanukkah Tale

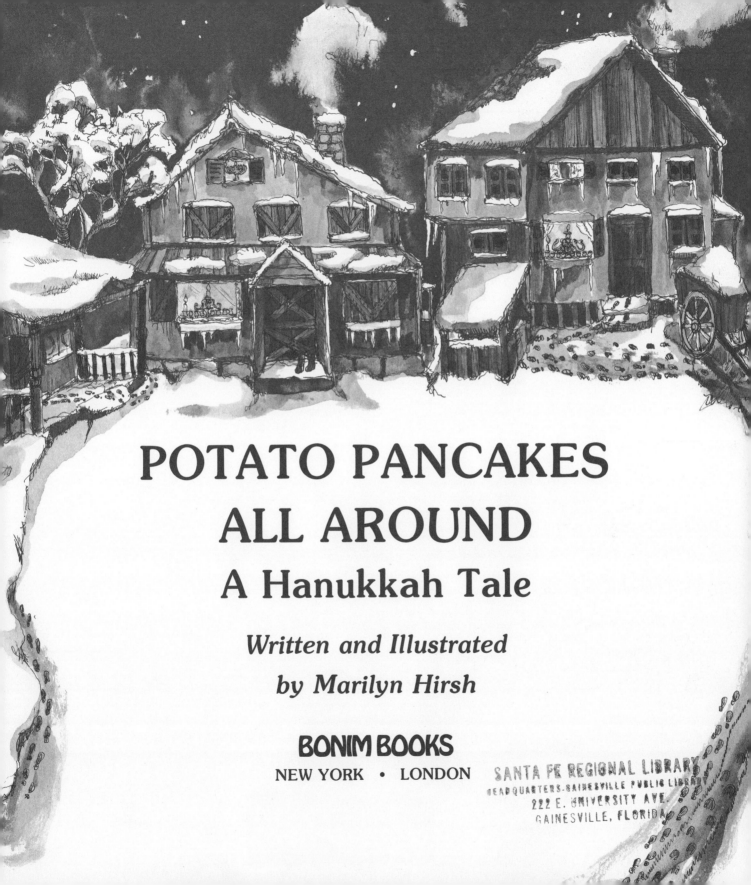

POTATO PANCAKES
ALL AROUND
A Hanukkah Tale

Written and Illustrated
by Marilyn Hirsh

BONIM BOOKS
NEW YORK • LONDON

TO JIM BY HIMSELF

Library of Congress Cataloging in Publication Data

Hirsh, Marilyn.
  Potato pancakes all around.

  SUMMARY: A wandering peddler teaches the villagers how to make potato pancakes from a crust of bread.
  [1. Hanukkah—Fiction] I. Title.
PZ7.H598Po   [E]   78-17927
ISBN 0-88482-762-3

BONIM BOOKS

a division of Hebrew Publishing Company
80 Fifth Avenue
New York, N.Y. 10011

Printed in the United States of America

On a cold winter afternoon, Samuel the peddler walked
down the road to a village.

He passed children sliding and sledding and skating.
"The children are out of school early," he said to himself,
"because tonight is the first night of Hanukkah."

When Samuel reached the village, it was almost dark. He knocked on the door of a house. Mama opened the door and smiled at the peddler.

"A guest is always welcome," she said. "Come in. We are just lighting the first candle."

So they all sang the blessings together.

The two grandmothers went to the stove.

"Aha," thought Samuel, "now they'll start making potato pancakes."

"We'll use my recipe," Grandma Yetta said firmly.

"No, mine is better!" answered Grandma Sophie.

"Who needs recipes?" said Samuel the peddler. "I'll show you how to make potato pancakes from a crust of bread!"

"Some say for potato pancakes a pickle, a fish, or a cabbage is good," Samuel continued, "but I say a crust of bread is best."

"Ridiculous," said Grandma Yetta.

"That's crazy," said Grandma Sophie.

"We're hungry!" cried the twins.

"So let's try the peddler's idea," said Mama.

Samuel took a bowl from his sack. "Who wants to hold it?" he asked.

"We do!" yelled the twins.

Samuel carefully grated a crust of bread into the bowl. "It looks delicious," he announced. "But it needs a little water."

The grandmothers wouldn't even look.

The peddler tasted the batter. "Some would say it needs salt . . . a little pepper, perhaps?"

"Even I know it needs salt and pepper," said Papa.

"Well, if you insist, I wouldn't say no," replied the peddler. And he added salt and pepper.

Samuel noticed a chicken looking in the window. "I think this chicken is trying to tell me something. But what could a chicken say?"

"I know!" cried Rachel. "The chicken is telling you to add eggs."

"I have heard of that," agreed the peddler. And he added six eggs.

"He takes advice from chickens," said Grandma Yetta.

"Do *you* have any suggestions?" he asked her politely.

"May you grow like an onion with your head in the ground!" she shouted.

"Ah, onions! A good idea," said Samuel.

So David hurried to chop some onions.

Samuel smiled. "Any minute now, we'll have potato pancakes."

"But what about the potatoes?" asked Sarah. "I grated all these potatoes, all by myself."

"It's not in my recipe," said Samuel, "but it's a sin to waste food. So what can it hurt? I'll add your potatoes."

And he did.

"What will you fry the potato pancakes in?" asked Grandma Yetta and Grandma Sophie at the same time.

"In a frying pan," answered Samuel. And he took one from his sack.

"Chicken fat is best," insisted Grandma Yetta.

"You may be right," said Samuel.

"Goose fat is better," declared Grandma Sophie.

"I wouldn't say no," Samuel replied.

So Samuel took a big spoonful of chicken fat and a big spoonful of goose fat and began to fry the potato pancakes. Delicious smells filled the house.

Samuel kept on frying. More and more potato pancakes piled up.

Finally, it was time to eat. So they ate and ate and ate potato pancakes all around. Even Grandma Yetta and Grandma Sophie agreed that the potato pancakes were the best ever.

And they danced.
And they sang.
And they played games until very late.
Grandma Yetta and Grandma Sophie
gave the children pennies.
Then everyone went to sleep.

The next morning, the family begged Samuel to stay for
the whole eight days of Hanukkah.

"Thank you," said Samuel, "but a peddler must move
along. I know you'll have a happy Hanukkah . . . now that you
can make potato pancakes from a crust of bread."

GRANDMA YETTA'S AND GRANDMA SOPHIE'S RECIPE FOR POTATO PANCAKES

(after all, not *everyone* can make them out of a crust of bread!)

Here's What You Need:

4 medium potatoes
1 small onion
2 eggs
2 tablespoons unflavored bread
  crumbs
1 teaspoon salt
½ teaspoon pepper
½ cup oil

vegetable peeler
grater
large mixing bowl
measuring cup
measuring spoons
tablespoon
frying pan
metal spatula
large plate or platter
paper towels

Here's What You Do:
1. Peel the potatoes and grate them into the bowl. Pour off the extra liquid into the sink.
2. Peel the onion and grate it into the bowl.
3. Break the eggs into the bowl. Add the bread crumbs, salt, and pepper. Mix very well.
4. Heat the oil in the pan on medium heat until it sizzles.
5. Carefully drop the batter into the hot oil by tablespoonfuls. Flatten each pancake with the spatula.
6. When the pancakes are golden brown, carefully turn them over with the spatula. Fry on the other side until brown and crisp.
7. Put 3 or 4 paper towels on the plate or platter. When the pancakes are done, use the spatula to remove them from the pan and place on the platter. The extra oil will drain onto the towels.
8. Now six people can enjoy them with applesauce or sour cream.

NOTE: An adult should be around to help with the grating and frying.

HANUKKAH

Hanukkah, the Festival of Lights, is a joyous holiday. The word *Hanukkah* means "dedication," recalling the rededication of the Temple in Jerusalem in 164 B.C.E., over 2,100 years ago. It commemorates the victory of the Maccabees over the Syrians who had tried to destroy the Jewish way of life. The celebration begins on the twenty-fifth of the Hebrew month of Kislev (November or December) and lasts for eight days.

After their victory, the Maccabees wanted to light the Temple *menorah* (candelabrum). They found enough pure oil for only one day. A story is told that, by a miracle, this oil burned for eight days until new oil could be prepared.

Today, a special menorah is lit on Hanukkah in Jewish homes all over the world. It has holders for a row of eight candles. Another holder, placed apart from the others, is for the *shamash*, the helper candle used each night to light the others. On the first night, the *shamash* and one candle are lit. One more candle is added each night for the whole eight days of the holiday. Hanukkah blessings and songs are sung.

Small gifts, coins, or candies are given to children. They are allowed to stay up late listening to the story of the Maccabees and playing games. A traditional Hanukkah game is played with a *dreidel*, a four-sided top.

The favorite food served on Hanukkah, called in Yiddish *latkes*, is—of course—potato pancakes.